THE BRITTLETON JOURNEY

GIA MARY PRADEEP

Copyright © Gia Mary Pradeep
All Rights Reserved.

This book has been self-published with all reasonable efforts taken to make the material error-free by the author. No part of this book shall be used, reproduced in any manner whatsoever without written permission from the author, except in the case of brief quotations embodied in critical articles and reviews.

The Author of this book is solely responsible and liable for its content including but not limited to the views, representations, descriptions, statements, information, opinions and references ["Content"]. The Content of this book shall not constitute or be construed or deemed to reflect the opinion or expression of the Publisher or Editor. Neither the Publisher nor Editor endorse or approve the Content of this book or guarantee the reliability, accuracy or completeness of the Content published herein and do not make any representations or warranties of any kind, express or implied, including but not limited to the implied warranties of merchantability, fitness for a particular purpose. The Publisher and Editor shall not be liable whatsoever for any errors, omissions, whether such errors or omissions result from negligence, accident, or any other cause or claims for loss or damages of any kind, including without limitation, indirect or consequential loss or damage arising out of use, inability to use, or about the reliability, accuracy or sufficiency of the information contained in this book.

Made with ♥ on the Notion Press Platform
www.notionpress.com

Contents

Preface

Welcome to The Brittleton Journey, a charming tale crafted by 11-year-old Gia Mary Pradeep. Set in the lively halls of Brittleton Towers, this story follows a group of spirited first-formers as they navigate friendships, pranks, and heartfelt adventures.

Inspired by her own imagination and experiences, Gia brings to life a world filled with laughter, mischief, and lessons that resonate with readers of all ages. Her storytelling captures the joys and challenges of childhood, reminding us of the magic in everyday moments.

Step into Brittleton Towers and join Gia on this delightful journey. We hope it leaves you smiling and inspired!

Acknowledgements

Writing The Brittleton Journey has been a remarkable adventure, and I am deeply grateful to everyone who made this book possible.

First and foremost, I would like to express my heartfelt gratitude to Dr. Swaminathan Krishna, Principal of Sanskara School, whose unwavering motivation and belief in my abilities inspired me to embark on this journey. A special thanks to our librarian, Ms. Nitha Varghese, for her constant encouragement and guidance throughout this process.

To my beloved Appa- Pradeep George and Amma- Nedha Pradeep; words will never be enough to express how much I love you both. Thank you for your unwavering support, for always standing by my side and for believing in me every step of the way.

To my little brother- Noe, your playful mischief and endearing charm have been a constant source of inspiration. You've added a special spark to this story, and for that, I'm forever grateful.

I would also like to acknowledge the role of ChatGPT, which served as a brilliant proofreading assistant, and the Bing Image Creation Tool, which helped bring the cover page of this book to life.

A special thanks to my batchmates from Jackwood, whose camaraderie, stories, and shared experiences have been an incredible source of inspiration for this book.

To all these amazing people, I dedicate this work with deep appreciation and love. Thank you for making The Brittleton Journey a reality.

CHAPTER ONE

THE BIG QUESTION

Patrica, Lucy, and Susan were three siblings living in Arizona, USA. The oldest, Patrica—often called Pat—was 14 years old, with blue eyes and a gentle smile. The younger two, Lucy and Susan, were 12-year-old twins. Like Pat, they had blue eyes, but they shared a mischievous, yet obedient nature.

It was a Saturday evening, and the siblings were playing chess.

"Only a few more days until school starts!" Lucy exclaimed. "I love it when school reopens—no homework, no classes, no anything on the first day!"

"Yeah, but the days after that are worse. MORE homework, MORE classes, MORE EVERYTHING!" groaned Susan.

"We don't even know if we're going to our old school!" Pat reminded them. "Mother has that conference she needs to attend, so she said she might send us to a boarding school."

The children's mother, Mrs. Joy, was a surgeon—a very good one, in fact. Her job often required her to attend "conferences" where she met other doctors and learned new techniques. Their father, Mr. Joy, was also a doctor, but he worked in Canada and rarely visited the family.

"BORING OLD BRITTLETON TOWERS!" Lucy and Susan screamed together.

"We don't want to leave all our friends here!" added Lucy.

"And who knows? There might even be MORE homework!" Susan chimed in.

"What's so great about it anyway?"

"Well," Pat began, "at a boarding school, we get to make new friends. Plus, we waste so much time doing homework after school because of the bus ride home. At boarding school, we'll have more time to finish it. And after all, Aunt Edith says it's a great school. So does Jane!"

Aunt Edith was their mother's sister, and Jane was her daughter. The siblings loved it when Jane visited, and Jane loved spending time with them too. Jane, a year older than Pat, was 15.

"Mom says that if we like Brittleton Towers, we can stay there."

"NOT A CHANCE!" Susan declared.

"I agree with Susan," Lucy said firmly.

"How will you even know if you like it if you don't try?" Pat asked. "You two are just a pair of solemn potato heads!"

"Prove it!" the twins demanded, almost in unison.

"Well, here are the facts!" Pat replied.

She grabbed a piece of paper, scribbled something down, and stuck it on the twins' bedroom door. She placed it high on the door, just out of their reach.

Facts:

1. They think all things are stupid.

2. They think all things are useless.

3. They can't solve -16 − 677.

4. They can't solve it because they are true, solemn potato heads.

"Hey!" shouted Susan.

"Not fair!" protested Lucy.

"We know that -16 − 677 is negative 661!"

"That's exactly why you're potato heads!" Pat teased. "The real answer is negative 693!"

"That was just a mistake!" the twins protested in unison.

They bolted after Pat, running around the bedroom. The twins chased, and Pat scrambled to escape. Suddenly, their mother barged into the room.

"What is all this noise? Don't make so much of it! I need to get everything ready for the conference," she scolded, before leaving the room again.

Mrs. Joy didn't notice the poster stuck to the door, so it stayed there, overlooked.

"Well, tonight at dinner, we need to ask Mom the big question," Pat declared.

"The big question?" asked the twins curiously.

"Yup! The question that will decide whether we go to boarding school or not."

CHAPTER TWO

A Glimpse of Brittleton

Pat winked at Lucy and Susan.

"Mum?" asked Pat.

"Yes, Pat?" replied her mother.

"Are we going to boarding school?"

"I haven't decided yet. I'll tell you my decision by tomorrow morning," Mrs. Joy said with a smile. "Anyway, I think you'll enjoy it there. There are many things you can try at that school. There are also clubs for various interests like sports, art, music, and nature."

"What other things are there?" asked Pat.

"Well, I've heard Jane say there's a huge library filled with many different books by various authors. You also have the chance to write your own book."

Pat's eyes widened. She had always wanted to publish her own book but never had the chance to do so.

"Well, as I said earlier, I'll let you know tomorrow," said Mrs. Joy. Then, she got up and left.

"What about that?" asked Pat. "This might be one of the best schools ever! Lucy, you can join the art club!"

Lucy was a very skilled artist and had won many art competitions.

"And Susan, you can join the sports club!"

Susan was very talented in sports, especially swimming. Both twins' faces lit up at this, but Susan was still indignant.

"I still DON'T WANT to go!" said Susan.

"Well, look at the bright side. I'll still be able to annoy you!"

They all laughed at this.

"I wonder what other things are there in this school," mused Pat.

"I heard Jane say there are different houses," said Susan. "Houses as in teams that compete against each other in house competitions. She told me there are four houses: Air, Water, Nature, and Fire. These houses are represented by different colors."

"Which house is Jane in?" asked Lucy.

"She's in Air."

"I hope we get to join Air too," said Pat.

"I agree," replied Susan. "If we're in different houses, it'll be difficult to compete."

"Well, we don't even know if we're joining this school," said Lucy. "I still don't want to go."

"Well, this is EXACTLY why you're a solemn potato head!"

Lucy pretended to turn into an angry bull, holding up two fingers on her head to mimic horns. Then she charged at Pat, who squealed, and they all fell together like a bunch of dominoes.

CHAPTER THREE

THE BIG DECISION

It was the day. The day Mrs. Joy would decide whether the children were going to boarding school or not.

"Children," called Mrs. Joy.

They all gathered in the living room, eagerly awaiting her decision.

"I've given this a lot of thought," Mrs. Joy began. "I even called Jane to ask her opinion. The final answer is yes—you are going to boarding school."

Pat and Lucy were thrilled. They were excited to see Jane, join the clubs, and find out which houses they'd be sorted into. They also looked forward to trying out new activities at Brittleton Towers.

Susan, on the other hand, felt the same excitement deep down but refused to show it.

"Also," added Mrs. Joy, "Jane will be coming this evening to tell you more about the school and help you prepare for your first day. School starts the day after tomorrow."

All three faces brightened at the news.

"JANE IS COMING!!!" screamed Lucy, her voice ringing with joy.

Susan joined in, just as excited.

"I hope she gets here quickly," said Susan.

"Me too!" said Pat.

"Calm down," Mrs. Joy interrupted. "Jane will be here soon enough. Tidy up your rooms before she arrives and make sure to give her a warm welcome."

"Of course!" Pat assured her, and the twins nodded in agreement.

Once Mrs. Joy left, the siblings hurried to clean their rooms.

"Let's finish quickly so we can spend the rest of our time planning what to do with Jane!" said Pat.

"Alright!" the twins replied.

After tidying up, they planned games to play with Jane and then had lunch. The hours passed slowly as they eagerly awaited her arrival. Finally, at 6:00 p.m., the doorbell rang.

Pat rushed to open the door, and there stood Jane.

"Jane!" shrieked the three siblings in unison.

"Pat! Lucy! Susan! How are you all?" Jane replied with matching excitement.

They ran to hug her, their happiness unmistakable.

"I'm so glad you came!" Pat exclaimed.

"Me too!" Jane responded with a big smile.

Once everyone settled down, Jane began talking about Brittleton Towers.

"It's the best school in the world," Jane said. "There are so many opportunities to explore new things. I'm sure Aunt Joy already told you about the clubs. And Pat, you might finally get a chance to write your own book. I know you've always wanted to."

"That's true," Pat admitted, her eyes gleaming.

"And Susan," Jane continued, "do you remember I mentioned the four houses?"

"Yup!" Susan said quickly.

"She told us about them," Lucy chimed in.

"Well, the most exciting thing is the grand program at the end of the year," Jane added. "Each form organizes an event without any help from the teachers and performs it in front of the parents."

"What if we mess up?" asked Lucy nervously.

"Nobody has, and nobody will," Jane reassured her. "This school changes people for the better—you'll see."

"I'm excited!" Lucy admitted. "I really want to go to Brittleton Towers."

"Me too," said Pat.

"I'm still not excited," Susan muttered. "I don't want to leave our old school."

Jane was amused by Susan's stubbornness.

"You know, Susan," she said gently, "even I didn't want to go to Brittleton Towers at first. But trust me, this school changes people for the better."

Susan stayed silent, still unsure, so they changed the subject.

"Who wants to play something?" Pat asked, trying to lighten the mood.

"Me!" Susan, Lucy, and Jane said simultaneously.

They spent the evening playing board games until it was time for dinner. Aunt Edith, Jane's mother, joined them for the meal. The family chatted happily, and afterward, the children and Jane watched a movie before bedtime.

The next morning, they were eager to start packing—well, all except Susan. After breakfast, Mrs. Joy handed them a list of things to pack.

"I've spoken to the headmistress of Brittleton Towers," Mrs. Joy said. "Her name is Mrs. Roberts, and she seems very nice."

"What forms are we in?" asked Pat.

"The school only admits students aged 12 and older," Mrs. Joy explained. "Lucy and Susan will be in the first form, while Pat will be in the third form."

"And I'll be in the fourth form!" Jane added excitedly.

"You'd better start packing," Mrs. Joy continued.

"Well, I'm going to Alice's house," Susan announced abruptly.

Alice was the twins' best friend and one of the reasons Susan didn't want to leave for boarding school. Without another word, Susan slipped on her shoes and left.

"Just give her some time," Mrs. Joy said with a sigh.

"Can I go to Alice's house too?" Lucy asked.

"You can," her mother replied. "Pat, you can go with her as well. But be back in an hour to finish packing."

"Thank you, Mother!" Lucy and Pat exclaimed in unison.

"Jane, you can come along too!" added Pat.

"All right!" Jane agreed cheerfully.

CHAPTER FOUR

FINAL PREPARATIONS

They rang the doorbell. Suddenly, the door opened, and there stood Alice—and a grumpy Susan.

"Lucy, you came!" squealed Alice.

"Alice! How are you?" asked Lucy.

The group of five went inside, where they were greeted by Boomer, Alice's energetic dog.

"Boomer!" Lucy squealed, her love for animals evident. "I wish we had a dog," she said, turning to Pat and Jane.

"Me too," said Jane.

"Well then," Alice said, "you're welcome to spend as much time as you want with Boomer!"

"Where are Mr. and Mrs. Willow?" Pat asked.

"They're out," Alice replied. "We can play all we want."

"Well, we only have an hour," Pat reminded them.

"Just an hour?" Susan muttered. "I don't want to leave in an hour."

"Mother's orders," Pat explained. "We still need to finish packing."

Susan's grumpy expression deepened, but they all played until the hour was up. Then Alice and Boomer walked them to their home.

"Come to see us before we leave tomorrow!" Lucy reminded Alice.

"Of course!" Alice promised.

"Bye, Boomer!" Lucy said enthusiastically.

"Woof! Woof!" Boomer barked.

"I'll take that as a goodbye," Jane said with a laugh.

They all laughed as they waved goodbye. When the siblings and Jane entered their house, they were surprised to see not just their mother, but also their father.

"Father!" the three children squealed in unison. "You're here!"

"Hello, Pat. Hello, Lucy. Hello, Susan. I came to see you all before you leave. I'll also visit during your half-term break," Mr. Joy said with a smile.

The children were overjoyed.

"Father, look! Jane is here too!" Lucy said, pointing toward her cousin.

"Hello, Jane!" Mr. Joy greeted warmly. "How are you? I haven't seen you in so long."

"I'm fine, Uncle Joy," Jane replied.

"I'm glad to hear that," he said.

"Now, all of you, start packing!" Mrs. Joy instructed. "Here's the list. You can also pack one board game and two books each for your free time—nothing more."

The children got to work and finished packing before lunchtime.

During lunch, Aunt Edith mentioned that she had baked some cookies for them to take along for the train ride to Brittleton Towers.

"Can we just taste one each now?" Jane asked eagerly.

"You can all have half of a cookie each," Aunt Edith replied. "You'll need the rest on the train."

They each took a cookie and broke it into halves.

"They're delicious!" Lucy exclaimed.

"I certainly agree," Susan said, her face lighting up. "I love them so much."

"Yum!" Pat added. "I love them too."

"It's Mum's specialty," Jane explained proudly. "She makes the best treats in the entire world."

After thoroughly enjoying the cookies and showering Aunt Edith with compliments, the children played a round of chess. When that match was over, they moved on to Monopoly, and then to Snakes and Ladders.

By the time they finished their games, it was dinner. After dinner, they all went to bed early, excitement buzzing in the air as they anticipated the day ahead.

CHAPTER FIVE

New Adventures Begins

They arrived at the train station. Pat, Lucy, and Susan were excited, but they also missed their friends—especially Susan. Noticing their gloominess, Jane decided to cheer them up.

"You'll love Brittleton Towers," she said. "On the first day, we can do whatever we like. At the end of the day, they'll give us our timetables and syllabus."

"How many exams do we have per year?" Lucy asked.

"Four," Jane replied. "Two worth twenty marks and two worth eighty."

"I hate exams," Lucy groaned.

"Me too," said Susan. "I just want to go back to our old school with Alice."

"Well, just give Brittleton Towers a try," Jane said gently. "I'm sure you'll like it."

"Are we going to be separated into different compartments by form?" Lucy asked.

"Yes," Aunt Edith replied. "But if people are from the same family, arrangements can be made so they can stay in the same cabin."

The siblings' faces brightened at this. Jane already knew, so she wasn't surprised.

After saying their goodbyes, they boarded the train and found their cabin. Inside, they saw a girl about Jane's age and two others who seemed only a few years younger.

"Felicity!" Jane squealed excitedly. "Lilly! You're here too! Is that Ella?"

"Jane!" one of the girls replied. "How are you? And yes, Ella finally joined Brittleton Towers!"

Jane turned to her cousins. "Pat, Lucy, Susan, meet Felicity—my best friend. She's in my form. Those two are Ella and Lilly. I already know Lilly, but I've only heard about Ella. She's new."

"Hello, Felicity! Hi, Lilly! Hello, Ella!" the three siblings said in unison.

Felicity seemed kind and friendly, and Ella, though shy, smiled at them. Lilly was smiling too.

"Hello!" the other three replied cheerfully.

"Felicity, these are my cousins," Jane continued. "That's Pat over there. She's going to be in the third form. And these two twins are Susan and Lucy—they'll be in the first form."

"How do you tell who's who?" Ella asked timidly, though clearly intrigued.

"Well, it's hard at first," Jane explained, "but Susan has dimples on both cheeks, while Lucy has one on her right cheek. Also, Lucy's hair is a slightly darker shade of brown."

"You're right!" Lilly said.

"I can see it too," Ella added with a smile.

The group settled down, but after a while, everyone grew bored.

"This train ride is going to be so long," Susan sighed, gazing out the window.

"Come on, Susan, it's not that bad," Jane said, smiling. "We can play games, read books, or even take a nap."

"I want to play games!" Lucy exclaimed. She pulled a deck of cards out of her backpack. "Anyone else?"

"Me!" Pat chimed in.

"Me too!" Lilly said.

As they played, Jane shared more about Brittleton Towers.

"You'll love the food there. They have the best scones and jam," Jane said.

"And the dorms are really nice," Felicity added.

"We'll even have our own common room!" Lilly said enthusiastically.

They continued playing cards and chatting. By the end of the train ride, Pat, Susan, Lucy, and Ella were feeling more excited than ever to see their new school—Brittleton Towers.

CHAPTER SIX

THE BRITTLETON TOWERS

"Look over there!" Lilly said excitedly. "That's Brittleton Towers!"

Before them stood a magnificent building—Brittleton Towers.

The newcomers were thrilled to see their new school and excited for all the adventures ahead. Pat, in particular, was looking forward to the house sorting. Jane was in the Air House, and Pat hoped to be sorted there too. She was also eager to see if she could find time to start writing her own book.

Ella was equally excited. She had always wanted to attend the school her sisters loved so much.

"What's the first thing we do when we get there?" Susan asked.

"Orientation," Felicity replied.

"Is it very long?" Lucy asked.

"No," Jane said. "Probably just about five to ten minutes."

Suddenly, the train came to a halt. They saw Brittleton Towers students disembarking, so they quickly gathered their belongings and stepped off the train as well.

At the station, children were grouped according to their forms. The form mistresses helped the students find their respective groups. Once everyone was off the train, it departed, leaving behind the excited chatter of students.

After forming groups, the children boarded carriages to reach Brittleton Towers. Although they could see the school from the station, it was too far to walk. Each form had two carriages, and the air was filled with lively conversation.

Jane and Felicity shared one carriage, Pat and Lilly were in another, and Susan, Lucy, and Ella rode together.

Lucy and Ella were chatting nonstop, quickly discovering they had a lot in common. Both of them were excellent at art.

"Looks like Lucy's already found a friend," Pat said to Lilly, glancing toward the first-form carriage. "Susan, though, looks a bit gloomy. Maybe she's missing Alice."

"She'll come around," Lilly said reassuringly. "Just cheer her up a bit. In a few days, she'll settle in. Who was your best friend back home?"

"Well, Lucy and I didn't have a particular best friend. We were just good friends with many," Pat replied.

Suddenly, they heard the sound of gates opening. It was the grand entrance to Brittleton Towers.

The children climbed out of the carriages and bustled around, marveling at their new surroundings.

The form mistresses led each group to their respective common rooms.

"Keep your luggage here and come to the orientation. You'll find your dorm later," said Mrs. William, the first-form mistress. "By the time you return, there will be a paper attached to the common room door listing all the students and their houses."

Mrs. William was a kind but strict teacher who wouldn't tolerate misbehavior.

The students then gathered in the auditorium. After the orientation by Principal Roberts, they returned to their common rooms.

Ella, Lucy, and Susan found out they were sorted into the Air House. The three were delighted. Jane, Felicity, and Lilly were already in Air House, so they weren't surprised. Pat came rushing over with a huge grin—she, too, had been sorted into Air House.

The group entered their common room. It was exactly as Lilly had described—cozy and beautiful. There was a staircase leading to a second platform, where the dorms were located.

Susan, Lucy, and Ella shared the same dorm. It had eight beds, meaning there would be eight students. A tall girl was already there, unpacking her things.

"Hello!" she said, looking up. "I'm Sarah. You must be new. The others in this dorm aren't new, though."

After the three introduced themselves, four more students arrived.

One of them was particularly cheerful, energetic, and lively.

"That's Jenny," Sarah said with a grin. "She's the class prankster."

Jenny pointed to another girl. "And that's Fiona. She's the class musician."

"And this is Hady," Jenny continued. "She's my best friend and an excellent prankster like me."

Jenny then motioned to a girl standing quietly. "And that over there is June, my cousin. She's the class brainiac," she said teasingly.

"I'm not a brainiac!" June protested.

"But you sure are smart," Sarah said with a smile.

After everyone finished unpacking, the eight girls chatted happily. They later went to the common room to meet the other first-form students.

Suddenly, an announcement rang out: it was time for supper. The children hurried to the dining hall.

"For supper, we'll have a grand feast," Fiona said. "Well, not very grand, but the food is delicious."

Sure enough, the meal was delightful. After eating, the students returned to their dorms, buzzing with excitement for the day ahead.

CHAPTER SEVEN

LIFE IN BRITTLETON

Several weeks had passed, and things were running smoothly at Brittleton Towers. Timetables had been handed out, and assignments were given to complete.

The head girl of the first form was a student from the second dorm named Amelia. Amelia was kind and sensible, and everyone agreed she was perfect for the role.

Each dorm also had a head girl to ensure the children followed rules, such as turning off lights and adhering to bedtime when the bell rang. In the twins' dorm, the head girl was Hady. While Hady was responsible and would make an excellent head girl, she occasionally indulged in pranks—but not as often as Jenny.

The other first-form dorm was headed by Amelia herself, as she was already the head girl of the form.

In Pat's form, the head girl was Ester, a student everyone liked and respected. Meanwhile, in Jane's form, the head girl was Jane herself. The three siblings felt incredibly proud when they heard this news.

The siblings and Ella worked hard to excel in their classes. Although the other students were trying as well, most of them weren't new and were already familiar with how the school operated.

Susan was feeling much better about the new school, but she still missed Alice at times.

Pat began writing her book, consulting with the librarian, who advised her to finish it before the annual day. The librarian explained that the book could be showcased to hundreds of parents during the event, offering a great start for her writing career.

Lucy joined the art club, and Susan and Ella joined her as well. However, Susan, not being particularly fond of art, also joined the swimming club.

Jane joined the nature club, along with Felicity and Pat. Lilly, who was in a different form, joined the music club. She had a remarkable talent for playing the violin, and her music brought joy to everyone who listened.

All the first-form students, including the twins and Ella, shared a class with the students from the second dorm of the first form.

Everyone managed to catch up with their lessons fairly quickly, except for Ella, who was struggling a little in Math. The twins often helped her in the evenings, tutoring her and helping her improve.

The first period for the first form that day was English. After breakfast in the huge dining hall, the students hurried to class.

Their English teacher, Mrs. Williams, was also their first-form mistress, as the twins had learned on reopening day. Mrs. Williams was an excellent teacher with beautiful cursive handwriting.

She had a talent for making complex grammar rules easy to understand and often shared helpful tips for memorizing them. She read literature chapters with such expression that it felt like the students were watching a live performance rather than just listening.

Additionally, she gave just the right amount of homework, understanding that her students had plenty of other demanding assignments from different teachers.

That day, the class read a chapter from Charlotte's Web by E.B. White. It was a touching story about a girl named Fern who saved a piglet named Wilbur. Wilbur went on to form a remarkable friendship with Charlotte, a spider who proved to be a terrific and selfless companion.

After English, they had Math, where Mrs. Ann began a new chapter on basic algebra. Mrs. Ann was a skilled teacher and explained concepts clearly. However, she was strict about homework and didn't tolerate incomplete assignments.

The rest of the day passed quickly, filled with several more periods. When lunchtime arrived, the students eagerly gathered in the dining hall. The food at Brittleton Towers was consistently praised as marvelous, and today was no exception.

After lunch, the students hurried back to their classes to continue their busy but fulfilling day.

CHAPTER EIGHT

THE GREAT WORKSHEET PRANK

Jenny and Hady were growing bored of their classes, so they decided to play a prank. They had a private meeting to plan their mischief.

"What prank should we play?" Hady asked in a mischievous voice.

"Well, I might just have a great idea," Jenny replied, smiling to herself.

"What is it?" Hady asked eagerly.

"Do you remember Mrs. Williams mentioning she'd conduct a worksheet on tenses?"

"Yeah," Hady replied.

"Well, we could swap the question paper with ridiculous questions! Since the rest of the students in our form aren't part of this plan, they'll laugh their hearts out when they see it," Jenny said, grinning.

"That's a marvellous idea!" Hady exclaimed, delighted. "We could even add some questions that might amuse Mrs.

Williams too."

"Excellent," Jenny said, clearly pleased with the plan.

The worksheet was scheduled for Wednesday, giving them enough time to forge fake question papers. Mrs. Williams always kept the worksheets in a drawer in the teacher's desk on the day of the test. If they could sneak into the classroom before breakfast, they could swap the papers.

The next day seemed to drag as Jenny and Hady eagerly waited for their chance. At times, they couldn't help giggling in class, which annoyed the teachers.

"What's so funny?" Mrs. Emma, the geography teacher, asked sternly when she caught them giggling during her lesson.

"Jenny, Hady, stand up and kindly tell the whole class what's so amusing," she demanded.

"Nothing's funny," Jenny said innocently.

"Then WHY are you giggling all the time?" Mrs. Emma retorted.

Mrs. Emma was a strict teacher who didn't appreciate jokes or misbehavior. She especially disliked students giggling in her class.

"Well, we told you, it's nothing," Jenny replied again, trying to keep her composure.

Mrs. Emma didn't like her response and was about to deliver a scolding when Hady stepped in.

"Mrs. Emma, we were just giggling about a joke we heard last Saturday. It was too funny for words. We're really sorry," Hady said quickly.

"Very well," Mrs. Emma said grudgingly. "But if I ever catch you giggling in my class again, you'll be reported."

"Noted," Hady replied before quickly sitting down with Jenny.

When Mrs. Emma turned to the board, Hady nudged Jenny.

"What on earth were you thinking?" she whispered. "Why did you talk to Mrs. Emma like that?"

"Well, doesn't one have the right to giggle?" Jenny whispered back. "I didn't like how she embarrassed us in front of the class."

"Mrs. Emma will always be Mrs. Emma," Hady replied. "But you need to work on your temper. Who knows what will happen next time if you giggle again?"

"You're right," Jenny admitted. "I'll apologize to Mrs. Emma after class. Thanks for standing up for me."

"Welcome," Hady said, admiring Jenny's willingness to apologize.

Finally, Wednesday arrived. Jenny and Hady successfully swapped the papers before breakfast. English was the first period after breakfast, so they didn't have to wait long to see the results of their prank.

The first formers ate their breakfast and hurried to class.

"Good morning, children," Mrs. Williams greeted as she entered. "Are you ready for your worksheet?"

"Yes, Mrs. Williams," the class replied. Jenny and Hady exchanged amused glances, trying hard not to burst into laughter.

Mrs. Williams began distributing the "worksheets," and as soon as the students read the questions, they glanced at Jenny and Hady, who looked perfectly innocent. The rest of the class, however, knew they were behind it.

Stifled giggles spread through the room as Mrs. Williams started reading the questions aloud:

Question 1: "What tense would you use to describe a talking cat's plans for world domination?"

Question 2: "Identify the verb conjugation for 'to burp' in the present perfect continuous tense."

Question 3: "Rewrite the sentence 'I ate a sandwich' in the future perfect tense, assuming you'll eat another sandwich next Thursday."

The puzzled look on Mrs. Williams's face was driving the students wild. Even Susan, Lucy, and Ella couldn't contain their laughter.

"And now, Question 5: 'If a time-traveling elephant were to attend a medieval jousting tournament, which tense would you use to describe its actions?'"

That was the last straw. The entire class erupted into uncontrollable laughter. Ella laughed so hard she fell out of her chair, and Sarah was wiping tears from her eyes.

Even Mrs. Williams couldn't help but smile. She gave a knowing look at Hady and Jenny, who exchanged a triumphant glance.

Their prank was a massive success.

CHAPTER NINE

TALENTS AND TITLES

It was Club Day, and everyone was rushing off to their clubrooms.

In the twins' dorm, most of the girls were in the drama club, except Fiona, who was in the music club, Ella and Lucy, who were in the art club, and Susan, who was in the swimming club. The head girl of the first form, Amelia, was also in swimming.

Though Lilly and Pat were in the same form, they had chosen different clubs. Lilly was in music, while Pat joined the nature club along with Jane, Felicity, and Ester, the head girl of the third form.

In the art club, they learned to make clay models. It was a lot of fun, and the art teacher, Mrs. Emily, was impressed by Lucy's work. Ella, too, showed remarkable talent.

Meanwhile, in the swimming club, the students completed five laps of each stroke.

"You swim really well!" Amelia said, impressed by Susan's perfect strokes. "You could join the swimming team!"

"Really?" Susan asked, her face lighting up. She was thrilled that Amelia, a member of the swim team, thought she was good enough.

Susan was starting to truly enjoy Brittleton Towers, even though she had hated the idea of coming at first. She remembered the fuss she had made at home about attending the school, but now, she had grown to like it. Still, there were moments when she missed Alice.

In the drama club, students were rehearsing for the school play, scheduled for the annual day at half term. Auditions had been held a week earlier, so the roles had already been announced.

It was a wonderful play, and Jenny and Hady had landed the lead roles as twin sisters—parts they seemed born to play.

June was proud of her cousin Jenny, though she herself had earned a very good role too. Sarah also got a notable part in the play.

The music club was equally exciting. They were also preparing for the half-term celebration. A solo performance was planned, with one student selected from each form. Fiona was chosen from the first form, while Lilly represented the third form. This didn't come as a surprise to anyone, given their talent.

The nature club had its own charm. That day, they took a scenic route on a nature walk, enjoying the breathtaking beauty of the surroundings.

When club time ended, the students returned to their dormitories. Being Sunday, they had no classes for the day.

By now, most people had almost forgotten about the prank, but whenever it was brought up, the first formers would burst into laughter.

"Our cousin Jane says the fourth formers think the prank was very clever," Lucy remarked.

This made the two pranksters feel proud.

"The look on Mrs. Williams's face was priceless," Sarah said. "Though it was kind of her to take it so lightly."

"It sure was," Jenny agreed. "If it had been Mrs. Emma, it would have been a completely different story."

Just then, Susan walked in, beaming. "Hey, guess what? Amelia said I'm good enough to be on the swim team!"

"That's amazing!" Hady exclaimed.

Everyone was thrilled for Susan.

"Now everyone in this dorm has a talent!" Jenny declared.

Suddenly, Jenny grabbed a piece of paper, scribbled a few things on it, and stuck it beside her study table. It read:

Sarah – The Voice of Reason (aka Sensible)

Jenny (me) – The Prank Mastermind

Hady – Partner in Crime

June – Brainiac

Fiona – Melody Queen

Ella – Artistic Genius

Lucy – Clay Model Maven

Susan – Swimming Sensation

"What's this for?" June asked, peering at the list.

"Just so I remember who's who, my dear cousin," Jenny replied with a grin. "Everyone is just getting too marvelous for words."

They all laughed.

Jenny giggled, admiring her handiwork. "I should make one for the whole school!"

Hady peeked over her shoulder. "Do it! But don't forget to include Mrs. Emma as The Stern Sentinel."

Jenny snickered. "Already on it!"

CHAPTER TEN

PAT'S BIG MOMENT

Half-term had finally arrived, and excitement buzzed through the school. Parents came to take their children out for the afternoon before the much-anticipated annual celebration later that evening.

Pat was thrilled—and nervous. Her book was going to be officially released, and the librarian, Mr. Thompson, had praised it highly.

Susan, Pat, Lucy, and Jane went out with Mr. Joy, Mrs. Joy, and Aunt Edith for lunch. They chose a cozy nearby restaurant so they could return in time for the celebration.

"How's everything back in Arizona?" Susan asked eagerly.

"Wonderful," Mrs. Joy said with a smile. "Alice misses you and has been asking about you. And Boomer is as energetic as ever."

Susan felt her spirits lift at the news, though she still missed Alice deeply.

After lunch, they returned to school, and Pat's excitement grew as the evening approached.

The celebration began with performances from each form.

The first formers performed a delightful play they had rehearsed for weeks. Jenny and Hady, playing twin sisters, were perfect in their roles, and the audience loved them. The third formers presented an energetic dance performance, and the fourth formers had everyone roaring with laughter during their stand-up comedy act.

Finally, the librarian took the stage, inviting Pat to join him.

"Ladies and gentlemen," Mr. Thompson began, his voice clear and warm. "Today, we celebrate not only the talents of our students but also the creativity of one of our own. I'm honoured to present Pat Joy's very first book!"

The hall erupted into applause as Pat stepped forward, her cheeks flushed with pride. She read an excerpt from her book—a story filled with adventure and humor. The audience hung on her every word, captivated by the vivid scenes she described.

When she finished, the applause was deafening. Her parents beamed with pride, clapping enthusiastically.

After the celebration, everyone lingered, chatting about the performances and congratulating Pat on her achievement. Even Lilly, one of Pat's new friends, joined in.

"That was incredible, Pat!" Lilly said. "I can't wait to read the whole book!"

Dinner that evening was lively, with laughter and conversation filling the dining hall. Everyone praised Pat's book and the first formers' play.

Back in their dormitory, the chatter continued.

"Pat, you were amazing up there!" Jenny said enthusiastically.

"Thanks, Jenny!" Pat replied, smiling.

The dorm gradually quieted as everyone drifted off to sleep, carrying with them memories of a truly special day—one that would remain unforgettable.

CHAPTER ELEVEN

Exam Fever and Exciting News

After half-term was over, the whole school was buzzing with exam preparations.

Every evening, the first formers gathered as a study group, diligently revising together. Nerves were high—especially for Ella, who seemed the most anxious of them all.

Everyone was looking forward to the ten-day vacation after the exams, a much-needed break.

This evening, the first formers were studying geography. They quizzed each other with flashcards from the chapter they had reviewed the day before.

"Name three major rivers that flow through Arizona," asked June, quizzing Lucy.

"The Salt, Gila, and Verde rivers," Lucy replied confidently.

"That's correct!" June said with a smile. "Excellent!"

Now it was Lucy's turn. "Name at least two states that border California," she asked Fiona.

"Arizona, Nevada, and Oregon," Fiona answered promptly.

"Good! You even named three," Lucy said approvingly.

They continued quizzing each other before moving on to math. After solving a few problems, they hurried to bed as Hady, the responsible dorm head, urged them.

"Hurry up! It's almost lights out!" Hady called.

They quickly tucked in and drifted off to sleep, knowing they needed to stay sharp for the next day.

The next day, classes continued as usual. The teachers were impressed by the first formers' determination to study. Even Amelia's dorm had formed a study group.

Mrs. Williams was particularly proud when she heard about the group sessions.

The first period was math with Mrs. Ann. She gave the students a revision exercise, and they performed well, thanks to their practice the night before.

"You've all done very well, class. Keep it up!" Mrs. Ann said warmly as she handed out the homework before leaving.

"Well, that was kind of Mrs. Ann," Amelia commented.

The others agreed.

The next period was French, taught by Mademoiselle Emily, who was French herself. French was easy for most students, as long as they remembered the verb conjugations.

Hearing footsteps outside, the class held the door open for the approaching teacher.

"Bonjour, Mademoiselle Emily!" the class greeted in unison.

"Bonjour, mes élèves! Comment allez-vous aujourd'hui?" she replied cheerfully.

"Nous allons bien, merci!" the class chorused back.

Sitting in the back, Ella whispered nervously to Susan, "I hope I don't mess up the verb conjugations today."

"Don't worry," Susan whispered back. "Just remember, lire and dire have different conjugations at vous."

"That's the part I always forget," Ella said.

"You'll get it right," Susan assured her with a smile.

Mademoiselle Emily began the lesson, writing on the blackboard. "Aujourd'hui, nous allons réviser les verbes réguliers. Can anyone give me an example of a regular verb?" she asked in English.

"Parler is an example, Mademoiselle," Sarah said, raising her hand.

"Bien, Sarah," Mademoiselle Emily replied with a nod.

After a few more classes, it was lunchtime. The first formers chatted excitedly as they made their way to the cafeteria.

Susan, Lucy, and Ella spotted Felicity walking down the hallway.

"Felicity!" the twins called, grinning.

"Twins! Ella!" Felicity greeted them warmly. "How are you all?"

"We're fine," the twins replied.

"Where's Jane?" Susan asked.

"She's coming," Felicity said with a smile.

"How's Ella doing?" Felicity teased, giving her a sly look. "Is she nervous about the exams?"

"Yeah, she's a bit nervous," Susan said, smiling at Ella.

"Just make sure she doesn't overwork herself," Felicity said kindly. "She tends to when exams get closer. I hear she's happy in the first form."

"She is," Lilly chimed in.

Suddenly, Jane and Pat joined the group.

"What's up, everyone?" Jane asked cheerfully.

"Lucy, Susan, I need to tell you something!" Jane said excitedly. "I already told Pat."

"What is it?" the twins asked, curious.

"Well, Mother said that you two and Pat can come to our house for the holidays—and each of you can bring a friend along!" Jane announced, her eyes sparkling.

The twins' faces lit up with joy. "That's the best news ever!"

Felicity added, "I've already written to our parents. I'm going with Jane, and Lilly is going with Pat. Mother said if Ella wants, she can go with you two."

Ella's eyes widened with excitement. "I do want to go! Really!" she said eagerly.

"Yes," Felicity confirmed. "You can come for three days."

The group was overjoyed. Jane was glad her cousins and their friends would be visiting. The twins and Ella couldn't stop smiling as they sat down for lunch.

When the other first formers heard the news, they congratulated the trio and shared in their happiness.

The next period was history—Mrs. Emma's class. The students groaned inwardly, as Mrs. Emma was known for being stern.

"Good morning, class," Mrs. Emma greeted as she entered.

"Good morning, Mrs. Emma," the students replied politely.

"Today, we'll discuss the American Revolution," Mrs. Emma began.

"Mrs. Emma, I have a question," Jenny said, raising her hand.

"Yes, Jenny?" Mrs. Emma asked, looking at her suspiciously.

"Would George Jefferson beat Puss in Boots at a game of chess?" Jenny asked innocently.

The entire class erupted into laughter, but Mrs. Emma was not amused.

"Jenny, what does that have to do with the American Revolution?" she asked, her face turning red with annoyance.

Jenny shrugged sheepishly. "I was just wondering, hypothetically."

Mrs. Emma sighed. "For your information, George Washington—not George Jefferson—might have been a good chess player. But Puss in Boots is fictional, so it's irrelevant."

The class laughed harder, and June added between chuckles, "George Washington and Thomas Jefferson are different people!"

Jenny smirked; she knew that already. It was all part of the joke.

"Enough with the jokes," Mrs. Emma said sternly and continued her lesson.

After dinner that evening, the first formers revised their French before going to bed. Hady ensured everyone was in bed before lights out.

The day had been busy, but as they closed their eyes, they were content—and ready to face whatever tomorrow would bring.

CHAPTER TWELVE

THE BUZZING PRANK

Several weeks passed, and the exams were finally over.

The top three results of each form were announced.

As expected, Jane came first in the form. Amelia came second. Jenny and Linda, a girl from the other dorm, tied for third place.

The others were happy with their rankings too. Ella was overjoyed; she did well and placed seventh, which was impressive, considering she was new.

Hady came in fourth, and Jenny was very happy for her.

Susan secured fifth place, and Lucy sixth. They were pleased to be near the top, especially since they were also new.

After the exams, the first formers celebrated. They were thrilled that they could go back home in just a week.

The other forms also celebrated. Their form mistresses were impressed with their grades. Even those who came in last had good overall scores.

Mrs. Williams was especially proud of the first formers, particularly the new students. Even those from Amelia's dorm performed well.

Jenny decided to celebrate with a prank. She didn't even tell Hady, so Hady could enjoy the surprise as well.

She lay in bed that night, pondering what prank to pull. Suddenly, an idea struck her.

What if I hide an alarm clock under the teacher's desk? she thought.

The teacher would try to figure out where the sound was coming from, driving everyone crazy. Jenny smiled to herself at the thought.

But I'll have to be careful. It shouldn't sound like the dispersal bell, she reasoned.

Then she remembered her alarm clock, which had a faint sound due to low batteries. It had almost failed to wake her up for class one morning.

If the sound is faint, it will be harder to locate, she thought. Plus, the clock's tone was different from the dispersal bell, so there'd be no confusion.

"This is perfect," she whispered to herself.

She decided to play the prank on Mademoiselle Emily. The Mademoiselle was lighthearted and loving, always laughing along when pranks were played. Jenny chose Thursday for her plan and soon drifted off to sleep.

Thursday came quickly. Jenny had taped the alarm clock under the teacher's desk before class. French was the first period, so she didn't have to wait long.

The door was held open as Mademoiselle Emily entered.

"Bonjour, mes enfants!" she greeted cheerfully.

"Bonjour, Mademoiselle!" the class chorused in reply.

Jenny had set the alarm to go off five minutes into the lesson.

While Mademoiselle Emily was writing the conjugation of a new irregular verb, a faint buzzing noise filled the room.

Mademoiselle turned around, speaking in English. "Does anyone hear that?"

The students nodded, except for Jenny, though no one knew where the sound was coming from.

Mademoiselle Emily looked around the room. "It sounds like a fly buzzing, but I don't see any flies," she mused.

The students began searching under desks and chairs, eager to help.

Jenny, struggling to suppress her laughter, had set the alarm to buzz for 10 seconds, pause for 5 seconds, then start again. She knew it would drive Mademoiselle Emily crazy.

As the buzzing paused, Mademoiselle sat back at her desk. Just as she did, the alarm went off again.

Mademoiselle jumped to her feet, exclaiming, "Ah ha! I'll find you, you pesky noise!"

Hady glanced at Jenny and saw the gleam in her eyes. It was a prank!

She quietly passed the word to the others, who stifled their laughter as they realized they'd been tricked too.

Mademoiselle Emily searched high and low, but the clock remained elusive. Finally, the entire class burst out laughing.

"What is the matter, mes enfants? Why are you laughing?" Mademoiselle Emily asked, bewildered.

The laughter only grew louder.

"It's a prank, Mademoiselle!" Amelia finally revealed.

Mademoiselle Emily's eyes widened in realization. "I got tricked!" she exclaimed. "You cheeky students! In France, no student would dare to do such a thing."

But then she smiled. These students! They play pranks, they misbehave, yet they are so caring.

She joined in the laughter, and the classroom rang with joy. Jenny's prank was a resounding success—a memory the first formers knew they'd cherish forever.

A FAREWELL FOR NOW

The day had finally arrived—it was the last day of school at Brittleton Towers. The air buzzed with excitement and a touch of chaos as students prepared to leave. They had just one hour before parents started arriving.

Susan could hardly contain her joy. Alice had written her a letter a few days ago, confirming she'd be joining Brittleton Towers next term. Lucy shared her excitement, her eyes sparkling with anticipation. Jane, Pat, and the twins were overjoyed too—Felicity, Lilly, and Ella would be staying with them for the holidays.

Pat, Lucy, and Susan were particularly thrilled about spending their first two holiday days with Mr. Joy—their father. No one felt sad about leaving school. They knew this wasn't goodbye forever, just a brief pause before they reunited for a new adventure.

The first-formers were buzzing in their dorms.

"Well, I guess this is farewell," Hady said with a dramatic sigh.

"Farewell for a few days, you mean!" Fiona shot back, laughing.

"At least we had a good laugh with all those pranks!" Ella said, smirking at Jenny and Hady, who exchanged knowing looks.

"They were hilarious!" Susan exclaimed.

The laughter echoed through the dorm, making the walls feel alive with the bond they'd built. They filed out of the dorms, their hearts light and full of hope for the holidays.

The dispersal scene was chaotic, as expected. Parents arrived in droves to collect their children, their voices mingling with the chatter of excited students. Those heading home by train rushed to gather their belongings and bid farewell to their friends.

Hady, Jenny, June, Ella, and the twins were among those traveling by train from their dorm. Ella's siblings, Jane and Pat, were also on board. The first-formers squeezed into one compartment, the energy in the air almost tangible.

As the train pulled away from the station, the excitement only grew. The scenery outside blurred into a swirl of greens and blues, but inside, laughter and chatter filled the space.

"I'm so glad Ella, Lilly, and Felicity can come and stay with us," Lucy said, her voice bright.

"And Alice is joining next year!" Susan added, her grin wide.

"What are you all planning for the holidays?" Ella asked, turning to Jenny.

Jenny's eyes twinkled mischievously. "Oh, I've got some big ideas. Hady's coming over to my house, and let's just say we'll be returning with pranks that'll make this term's tricks look like child's play!"

Hady laughed. "They'd better watch out—we're going to be unstoppable!"

The group burst into laughter, the sound carrying through the corridor.

Suddenly, Jane appeared at the door. "Anyone hungry? We've got chips and toffees!"

"Yes, please!" Susan said eagerly, and soon the compartment was full of crunching and the rustle of wrappers.

Moments later, the train began to slow. Pat, the twins, and Jane leaned out of the window as the station came into view.

"There's Aunt Edith!" Susan exclaimed, waving frantically.

"And there's Mother!" Pat shouted.

"I see Father too!" Lucy added, practically bouncing in her seat.

The four children rushed off the train, greeted by warm hugs and eager smiles.

"We've got so much to tell you about Brittleton Towers!" Lucy exclaimed.

"It was amazing," Susan added with a dramatic flourish.

"It was very amazing," Lucy corrected, nodding emphatically.

Mrs. Joy smiled, shaking her head. "And to think, you didn't want to go, Susan!"

"Well, Alice is coming next term, so it'll be even better!" Susan replied confidently.

Mr. Joy chuckled. "I'm glad you've found a home there. It sounds like quite the adventure."

"Well, it's goodbye to Brittleton Towers for now!" Jane declared with a grin.

But as they stood on the platform, the thought hung unspoken in the air: what new surprises awaited them next term?

And with that, it was goodbye to Brittleton Towers—just for now.

www.ingramcontent.com/pod-product-compliance
Lightning Source LLC
Chambersburg PA
CBHW031637170726
47990CB00017B/1411